For Pierre

Did you know that owls have very special eyes?

Maybe that's why Woo Hoo the owl could see the good in everyone.

When Woo Hoo swooped around the birch forest, he wasn't looking for lunch. He was looking for woodland creatures who did not yet know how awesome they were. Blurting out compliments was Woo Hoo's favourite hobby.

There was the time Woo Hoo spotted Nugget the hedgehog, all curled up on a prickly ball.

Nugget was feeling a bit small.

"Nobody notices me," Nugget sniffled, "because I'm so little."

"But your littleness is adorable!" beamed Woo Hoo. "Please don't hide all that cuteness in a prickle pocket!"

Nugget's little face popped out of his ball. "You think I'm cute?" the little hedgehog asked.

"You are the cutest creature in the whole forest!" Woo Hoo cheered, "WOO HOO! WOO HOO!"

Nugget felt a whole lot better.

Hopkins the rabbit was having a rough day. Whenever she hopped around the forest, her long ears flopped over her face.

"My ears are ridiculous," Hopkins pouted.

"Ridiculous?" Woo Hoo repeated. "But your ears are your coolest feature!"

"They are?" Hopkins said, twitching her nose curiously.

"You could hear me coming before I even got here!" the owl gushed. "Your long ears help you do amazing things!"

"I never thought of it that way," Hopkins perked up.

"You are the most alert creature in the whole forest!" Woo Hoo cheered, "WOO HOO! WOO HOO!"

Hopkins felt a whole lot better.

Nickels the Beaver sighed as he watched his reflection in the water.

"I am a goofy-toothed nincompoop," Nickels moped. "Maybe I should stop smiling."

"Please don't do that!" Woo Hoo begged. "You should be proud of your teeth!"

"Why?" Nickels shrugged.

"It is quite impressive that such a little guy like you can chop down a tall birch all by yourself," Woo Hoo said, clapping his wings.

Woo Hoo's compliment made Nickels smile with his nifty beaver teeth.

"You are the hardest working creature in the whole forest!" Woo Hoo cheered, "WOO HOO! WOO HOO!"

Nickels felt a whole lot better.

Woo Hoo found Zany the loon floating all alone on the lake.

"It's magical how your eyes turn red in the summer!" Woo Hoo gushed.

"It's nice of you to notice," Zany yodelled sadly, "because usually I just get laughed at."

"I can't imagine why anyone would make fun of such a stunningly beautiful bird."

"Everyone thinks I'm crazy," Zany explained, "because of my wacky yodel. And because I walk funny on land."

"CONGRATULATIONS on getting your picture on the Canadian coin!" squealed the happy owl. "Now everyone will see what a dazzling bird you are!"

"They chose ME?" Zany asked with wide, red eyes.

"You are the most famous creature in the whole forest!" Woo Hoo cheered, "WOO HOO! WOO HOO!"

Zany felt a whole lot better.

Snoop the racoon was sitting dismally on a rock by the lake.

"What colour is the sky?" the glum racoon asked the swooping owl. "I can't see colour. And that sometimes makes me sad."

"It's a lovely shade of blue today," Woo Hoo answered.

"It must be fantastically pretty," Snoop said, drying her tears.

"Look on the bright side!" chimed Woo Hoo. "Your vision may not be the best but you make up for it by being so resourceful! You can open things with your finger-y hands! You can find food just about anywhere! You can even figure out puzzles!"

"Well, there's that," nodded Snoop.

"You are the cleverest creature in the whole forest!" Woo Hoo cheered, "WOO HOO! WOO HOO!"

Snoop felt a whole lot better.

Momo the moose thought he was hiding. But Woo Hoo had no trouble spotting the mighty moose with his head sticking out from a grove of trees.

"You can't see me," Momo said. "I'm hiding."

"That's a shame," said Woo Hoo as he perched on Momo's antlers. "How can anyone admire you if you are hiding?"

"I'm just too big and cumbersome," Momo said, lowering his great head in shame.

"But that's what makes you so impressively strong!" the owl praised. "Only YOU can hold your head up proud with such a heavy rack of antlers!"

"My antlers are pretty groovy," Momo said with his eyeballs lolling up at his majestic paddles.

"You are the strongest creature in the whole forest!" Woo Hoo cheered, "WOO HOO! WOO HOO!"

Momo felt a whole lot better.

A stinky stench wafted around a hollow log. Embarrassed, Stinker the skunk was pretending the stinky stench was not coming from him.

"Stinker, you are an inspiration!" Woo Hoo bubbled.

"Me?" Stinker asked, scratching his head. "But the only thing I'm good at is smelling bad."

"Which is why nobody ever picks on you!" the owl said fondly. "All you have to do is lumber along and all the big meanies just run away! You have a special, stinky superpower!"

"Well shucks, Woo Hoo," said Stinker bashfully. "You sure know how to make a skunk feel less stinky."

"You are the most respected creature in the whole forest!" Woo Hoo cheered, "WOO HOO! WOO HOO!"

Stinker felt a whole lot better.

Up in a tree, Snuffles the cinnamon bear clung tightly. Woo Hoo perched on a nearby branch.

"It's so nice to see you up here, Snuffles!" the owl hooted.

"I climbed up here to avoid the other animals," Snuffles whispered. "I don't like the reddish colour of my fur. I wish I had sleek fur like my black bear cousins."

"But Snuffles," the wise owl said, "being a cinnamon bear is what makes you unique! You wouldn't want to blend in with all the other bears, would you?"

"I guess it's nice to be named after such a sweet spice," Snuffles blushed.

"You are the sweetest, most cinnamon-y creature in the whole forest!" Woo Hoo cheered, "WOO HOO! WOO HOO!"

Snuffles felt a whole lot better.

Chippy the chipmunk scurried nervously.

"Oh dear, oh dear, oh dear," Chippy chattered with his cheeks full of acorns. "I'm never going to be ready on time!"

"You amaze me, little Chippy!" Woo Hoo said to the anxious rodent.

"How so?" Chippy asked quizzically. "I'm a nervous wreck!"

"But you are such a great planner!" the owl observed. "Look at you packing away those acorns in your cheeks! Winter isn't for another six months and you are already thinking ahead! Good for you!"

Chippy relaxed a little. "Now that you mention it, I've never run out of acorns before. Maybe there isn't anything to worry about."

"You are the most responsible creature in the whole forest!" Woo Hoo cheered, "WOO HOO! WOO HOO!"

Chippy felt a whole lot better.

Yes, Woo Hoo made every creature in the birch forest feel good about themselves.

But sometimes even owls can have a bad day.

From up in her tree, Snuffles noticed Woo Hoo in his nest. His eyelids were sad and droopy.

"Oh no!" Snuffles called down to Nickels. "I think Woo Hoo is feeling glum!"

"I'll tell the others!" Zany yodelled, letting his voice echo across the water.

Before long, every creature in the birch forest had gathered together to form a plan.

Woo Hoo turned his feathery head all the way around and found the woodland creatures looking up at him in the tree.

"Friends?" Woo Hoo said. "What are you all doing here?"

"We're here to cheer you up!" squealed Nugget.

"Your big, yellow eyes are gorgeous!" cheered Hopkins.

"You can fly like an acrobat!" cheered Nickels.

"You are very wise!" cheered Zany.

"You see the beauty in everything!" cheered Snoop.

"You make me feel good about myself!" cheered Momo.

"You smell really good!" cheered Stinker.

"You are a great friend!" cheered Snuffles.

"You are the KINDEST creature in the whole forest!" cheered Chippy.

Then all the creatures cheered, "WOO HOO! WOO HOO!"

And Woo Hoo the owl felt a whole lot better.

Annelid Press